# Dare to Change

## By Jacqueline James

Dare to Change

# Dare to Change

## By Jacqueline James

# Table of Contents

Chapter 1:          Gods Test

# Chapter 2:    God's Challenges

# Chapter 3:        God's Blessings

# About the Author

Jacqueline James is a talented author with a 5-star rating. Jacqueline specializes in poetry and children's stories to bring to (you) the readers a quality of art that (you) can forever treasure. Jacqueline's main objective is to leave (you) the readers with a sense of peace and serenity that can cultivate throughout (your) daily encounters. She has written several books with each one containing genuine expressions of humility.

Jacqueline is extremely grateful that (you) have chosen her published books as part of (your) reading material.

# The Dedication

This book is dedicated to my first-born son.
Cedric Carl Haynes Jr.
Cedric has successfully demonstrated a sufficient amount of change. His amazing strength during the unforeseen challenges he faced has been the inspiration for this book.

# Introduction

This book "Dare to Change' is designed to help (you) to identify with certain areas of (your) life that may possibly be hindering (you) from succeeding. The author chose carefully selected poetry to present these scenarios. After each chapter blank pages for notes have been included to help (you) keep track of (your) progress. Allow the messages to penetrate (your) thoughts as they generate a revelation for change.

\

# Chapter 1

## Gods Test

## "Right-now Change" …

If you get caught up in a runt and things aren't
going your way,
Make a "right-now change", for your first day,

This will be the first day of the rest of your life,
So change the way you choose to fight,

You need to try something different to get
something new,
Until you find whatever's that's right for you,

It might be the best day of your life,
Or it might be an experience that you don't like,

Either way it's going to be up to you,
To approach life with a different attitude.

# **The Key…**

I took loyalty, hard work, commitment, perseverance,
dedication, and faith,

Mixed it together stirred it up thoroughly then I came up
with a blessing, that was the key to open my gate,

I made sacrifices and compromises,
While rationalizing and strategizing,

I brought them together while developing
Useful materials from my establishments,

Reaping all its rewards,
Was ultimately my final score.

# A Wise Man...

A wise man who learnt to listen,
Did less talking and became more attentive,

Nothing less than knowledge did he
desire,
With great wisdom he delivered the messages that he
acquired,

The information he shared made perfect sense,
Because, the importance of teaching he insist,

As the days ahead came to pass,
The words he spoke were sure to last,

Next this same wise man took to silence,
And, kept his peace to avoid any violence,

He hibernated for months to years,
While the outside world lived in fear,

Those who followed his prestigious plan,
Once again met up with the man.

# Lost and found...

Sometimes you have to lose yourself in order to find
yourself,
Let your situation resolve itself,

Deflecting your energy to someone else,
Can take the pity away from yourself,

Don't look back and don't think twice,
Find comfort in your own advice,

The moments that pass have expired,
To leave you with hope to be inspired,

Loss yourself in order to be found,
Then your true calling will be your rebound.

# **Life Pieces...**

Life pieces provided,
Never equally divided,

Poor people have nothing but other people's pieces,
Maybe a stolen or borrowed piece,
Nothing ever owned to say the least,

Nothing ever to call their own,
Never knowing where they belong,

Rich people have a large collection of valuable pieces,
Everything that's original and custom made,
With an authentic signature that will never fade,

Everything purchases for their special needs,
Acquiring lots of things for their personal greed,

Middle class people have a lot of scattered mix-match
pieces,
They hold onto everything they get, which makes them the
hoarding species,

They never let anything go when they're done with it,
They just pile up more and more stuff and never quit,

# Dare to Change

When their pieces are lost or shattered,
Sometimes they forget about the things that matters,

They draw themselves into their pieces,
Then their touch with reality, starts to decrease,

There's always plenty of life pieces provided,
But they will never ever, be equally divided.

# No More Secrets…

Everything will reveal itself in time,
From your secret-to their secrets-to mine,

What once was hidden and hard to find,
The viewers clearly will no longer be blind,

Once your eyes are open wide,
Then you'll be able to recognize,

It's time we all start to realize,
Once our own truths are revealed before our eyes,

Then there'll be no more secrets or no more lies,
There will be no more truths for us to hide,

Or no more secrets for them to find.
The truth will set you free without compromise.

# Going Higher…

I'm going higher and higher,
I can't do nothing but go higher,


I refuse to go anywhere but higher,
There's nothing left to do, but go higher,


Once I reach the top I won't come down,
I can't come down,


I'll refuse to come down,
I not capable of coming down,


I won't know how to come down,
I refuse to come crashing down,


I'm staying up,
I have evolved!

# **Unresolved issues...**

Problems are issues unresolved,
Things that we refuse to address or solve,


Stop trying to eliminate, remove, or go around,
Face them head on then your strength will be found,


When you're faced with problems that are challenging, and
hard,
Just take them to the 'alter', and leave them with the Lord,


Jesus died in order to casted all of our cares onto him,
So we could live our life's free of fear,


He wanted to leave us with a peace of mind,
That will last forever surpassing all time,

He never wants us to give up on life,
He want us to hold fast to his 'words', and fight with strive,

When you're faced with challenging from all of life
pressures,
They're not problems they're just unresolved issues.

# **Elevation...**

I need for you to listen, now please pay close
attention,
There's something that I much mention,

Once I elevate things will be different,
I worked hard I was relentless,

Pushing to the top was my intentions,
I sacrificed my days and worked on through my
nights,

I didn't stop until I got it right,
I made it to greater heights,

I did stuff some people couldn't comprehend,
When I gave up socializing with my old friends,

I don't have to solicit on the street corners again,
I'm only going to network for new beginnings to begin.
.

# A friend in me...

I was looking for a best friend I even made a wish,
I but after the process of elimination I was at the top of my
own list,

I was searching the world for a best friend,
It was me all along I am the best I can give,

I'm loving every minute of it I wouldn't trade me for the
world,
I am my one and only-my favorite girl,

I ask me for my own advice,
I follow it closely being very precise,

I ended up with the best friend ever,
It was "yours-truly", and I chose me forever.

# **Empty Land...**

I just don't quite understand,
Why all these people are homeless, with all this empty
land,

This could've been in God's perfect plans,
This is some selfishness imposed on by a man,

They want to keep everyone under an economical structure,
that's doomed to fail,
But if they lived off the land things will turn out well,

I know that there's disease and famine everywhere,
But it can be avoided if more people cared,

I'm aware it's a lot of homeless children that's on their own,
However there's also a lot of kind people that's willing to
give them a home,

It's put in place that you have to adopt a child,
So the economy can make money that's worth its while,

Most families can't afford it, or they don't qualify,
When they want to care for a child they get denied,

The child is placed in an orphanage until they become an
adult,
They're release into society with a few measly bucks,


What good is it doing to allow them to fend for
themselves?
They become a menace to society if nothing else,

Without any friends or family to show them the way,
They end up homeless at the end of the day,

Now, we're back to all this empty land,
That can be filled with 'habitats', on demand,

If we're willing to stick to God's perfect plan!

# **My Mission …**

If you didn't like what I did yesterday,

If you don't like what I'm doing today,

Then get out of my way for tomorrow,
If you try to avoid hating me, it going to be hard,

Because I'm on a personal crusade to serve the Lord,

I'm on a mission to share God's word,
It's the most precious words, that I've ever heard,

I'm on a mission to show love throughout my life,
To lead those who care to Jesus' light,

To teach you about God's mercy for your sorrows,
To leave you with hope for your tomorrows,

My mission is to remind you of God's good grace,
How He will bless you, as He did for me, through the trials
you face!

# Slam the door...

Slam the door on depression,
Slam the door on obsession,

Slam the door on defiance,
Slam the door on noncompliance,

Slam the door on defeat,
Slam the door on incomplete,

Slam the door on hast,
Slam the door on waste,

Slam the door on negativity,
Slam the door on captivity,

Slam the door on failure,
Slam the door on bad behavior,

Slam the door on violence,
Slam the door on rowdiness,

Slam the door on debate,
Slam the door on hate,

# Dare to Change

Slam the door on stealing,
Slam the door on killing,

Slam the door on egotistic,
Slam the door on statistics,

Slam the door on resistance,
Now open up the door to persistence,

# I'm Going to Leave You Alone…

My role as a mother is not to leave you alone,
Until I'm sure that you can stand on your own,

Right now, your life is going all too wrong,
I can hear you in my head singing the same old song,

But since you ask me nicely, I must step aside,
To see if you have what it takes to survive,

I know I taught you right from wrong,
I pray you should be able to survive on your own,

Don't allow your weakness to pull you down,
From whatever look good that comes around,

Be not tempted but stand your ground,
Hard work, and patience will keep you sound,

Now, I'm going to leave you alone,
Be at peace, as you stand strong.

# **Father's …Day…**

Fathers are as important as our Lord, has given,
Because of their presence we are all living,

They were created in the image of our God,
He allowed them to reproduce a wonderful, newborn child,

They were the beginning of life in the form of a man,
To reproduce life to meet God's demands,

Their purpose is to replenish the earth with the seeds, from
'Our Father',
Fathering new miracles, every second of the hour,

God has blessed them to be head-of-the-house,
Honoring the Lord's word, for 'He', is their boss,

They work hard to satisfy life's situations,
With lots of integrity, and complete dedication,

Always making their family their first priority,
With great sacrifices, never telling the world their whole
story,

We appreciate the 'Fathers', who care for their families, in
a unique and special way,
Every day we honor them as they continue to pray!

## **Unseen Tears...**

I've lived with the same anguish for several years,
Hopelessly trying to hold back my unseen tears,

I knew in my heart I had nowhere else to go,
My pain was hoovering, and my relief was slow,

I held on desperately to the possibility of one day becoming
free,
Perhaps my pain would seep through the cracks for the
world to see,

The tone in my voice was low and subtle when I spoke,
If you met me, I wasn't the same as the other folks,

I put on a happy face, to start my day,
Longing for the sun to shine my way,

Did anybody notice or sense my fear?
Behind my smile was unseen tears,

I wore the appropriate attire for every occasion,
I was suitably acknowledged through my conversation,

I would only address the issues that was presented before

Dare to Change


me,
I served as the president on the broad of a local committee,

I interact with people, on so many different levels,
Were they that deceptive or was I just that clever?

Could they see my abuse that have been lingering for years,
Beneath my professional image was unseen tears,

It's easy for you to ask, "why didn't I just leave?"
Trust me it wasn't that simple this you must believe,

My whole existence evolved around this 'Mr.'s life,
I wasn't no one at all if I wasn't the 'Senator's wife',

I kept the persona that all was well,
The paparazzi enforced it all their pictures would tell,

I'd be a public spectacle in my voice if they could hear,
That I was just another victim with unseen tears,

I gathered my pain, and tucked it up in my thoughts,
No one ever notice there was never a doubt,

Now, my worries were over when the world seen my 'tear',
There wasn't any more pain, and there wasn't any more
fear,

Eventually my tears came to its dreadful end,
Once I buried my husband, I was free from his sins.

# **Forgive me Lord…**

Forgive me Lord,
Going through life is sometimes hard,

Thank you, Jesus for not turning me over to the will of
my enemy,
Thank you, Jesus, for always having plenty of love for
me,

Forgive me Lord, for the sins that I have committed,
May they have been through commission, or
omission,

Thank you, Lord, for always being a God of second
chances,
I will honor with my whole heart your commandments,

Forgive me Lord, remove anything that's unpleasing
to your eyes,
Revive me Lord, make everything in me worthy, so
that my faith in You will survive,

Forgive me Lord, for the blasphemy committed with
my tongue,
Draw near Lord, so that I may be closer to Jesus,
your living son,

Dare to Change

Forgive me Lord, as I go through my days, with trials,
and tribulations,
Bless me Lord, so that I may have a closer spiritual
relation,

Forgive me Lord, as I may have 'envious' over my
neighbor,
Keep me Lord, through your 'grace', show me favor,

Forgive me Lord, for all the things that I may do,
Bless me the Lord, so that I may have a closer walk
with you!

## Notes with Incentives

## Notes with Incentives

## Notes with Incentives

# Chapter 2

## *God's Challenges*

1. Millon to Infinity …

2. His Behavior…

3. I Don't want to talk about…

4. Family Begin With …

5. Crystal …

6. It Might….

7. What it appears to be…

8. It is…

9. What's Left…

10. Black-Stripes…

11. Thanks for Giving…

12. Comfort Zone …

13. The 'Thrill' of You …

14. Retain Our Sons…

15. If I Could Be….

16. Ruthless…

17. On Point…

Dare to Change

**1 million to Infinity…**

It's 1 million to Infinity different things to do,
Try them all, one will be just right for you,

Be selective when you go about your day,
Make your time count, do things
your way,

If the first thing you choose doesn't work, then try
something else,
Whatever you do give it your best,

Don't use substitute or settle for less,
Keep moving forward to pass life's test,

Don't you dare look back on yester-years,
It's a waste of time and a waste of tears,

Try something new and if by chance you fall,
Pick up your pieces and humbly stand tall,

It's a million to infinity different things to do,
Find the one that's just right for you.

# His Behavior…

You weren't doing the world a favor,
By excusing his file and reckless behavior,

While he was exploring his sexuality,
He was distributing others reality,

He was in control of his every move,
His action was inexcusable and also cruel,

They change the course of so many lives,
Leaving young women unworthy, to become a wife,

You observed it all on a personal level,
You thought by not getting involved it made you clever,

But you were wrong you were very much involved,
You heard the screams clear and loud,

You are just as guilty as the perpetrator,
If you don't address it now, you'll address it later,

## Dare to Change


34


There are so many victims with so many scars,
They're some mother's-daughter, but they're not yours,

It didn't matter to you what condition they were left in,
Rather they survived or not their peace, still ended,


Now you're nonchalant saying "what's done is done"
You can't unring a bell when the bell has rung,

After he was done by his wicked behavior,
He discarded them all for our Lord to save them.

# I don't want to talk about it…

I don't want to talk about it,

I don't want to talk about all of the prejudice and the hate,
I don't want to talk about the country, always in a debate,


I don't want to talk about it,
All the limitations and restrictions that they put on a human being,
To keep them bounded, and shackled behind the scenes,


I don't want to talk about it,
How they keep them feeling inferior and always in doubt,
To deprive them from the basic necessities and watch them go without,


I don't want to talk about it,
How we can trample on each other's human rights,
I don't want to talk about it,
In order to live peaceful we have to fight,


I don't want to talk about it,
How we're always at 'War',

## Dare to Change

I don't want to talk about it,
How if we find freedom through chivalry, we must travel
far,


I don't want to talk about it,
How the same people we vote for, to enforce and instill the
law,
These are the same people who denied us the 'First
Amendment', and keep our 'backs', up against the wall,


I don't want to talk about it,
How a certain 'race', of people or still being sold into
slavery, in the 21st century,
I don't want to talk about it,
How the government allow these situations to go
unreported and refuse to be mentioned,


I don't want to talk about it,
How everyday thousands of innocent children are being
used and abused,
I don't want to talk about it,
How society avoids mentioning it on the evening news,


I don't want to talk about it,
How people rally together, and protest for civil rights,
equal rights, gay rights, and even human rights,
But behind closed door, they won't even do what's right,


I don't want to talk about it,
How poverty, and famine has stricken millions of lives,
I don't want to talk about it,

## Dare to Change

How disease and suffering has plagued many, from day to
night,


I don't want to talk about it, how basic health care is
overpriced, where no man could afford to relieve his own
suffering,
I don't want to talk about it,
How the same suffering was created, through men greed
and destruction,


I don't want to talk about it,
How everything is for sale, including salvation for men,
just to earn a buck,
I don't want to talk about it,
How the lottery and other get rich schemes or put in place,
to press our luck,


I don't want to talk about it,
How we live in one of the richest countries in the world,
yet one-third of the population lives in poverty,
I don't want to talk about it,
How children are starving, and their parents, try to survive,
by committing arm robbery,

# Dare to Change

38

I don't want to talk about it,
How mothers are selling her own babies, into prostitution
just to get 'high',
I don't want to talk about it,
How young children are committing suicide, with no will to
live-they rather die!

I don't want to talk about it,
These subjects, that are too hard, to talk about,
Because, you don't want to talk about it!

## **Family Begins With…**

Families begin with love, and listeners,
Devoting their time, to address life's issues,

Putting their hearts out on a limb,
To satisfy their emotions from within,

They're formed through all shapes and sizes,
From every race, age, and ethnicity-you'll be surprised,

They often wear their feelings on their sleeves,
They'll sacrifice everything, for what they believe,

They're always willing to help each other, when times are hard,
They'll pray together for strength, from Our Lord,

They'll be there to support each other, through every 'crazy', dreams,
And will work diligently to help each other, by any and every means,

Sometimes families, are not related at all,
Life situations bring them together both large and small.

# Dare to Change

## **Crystal...**


Crystal clear revealing things that are not there,

Now dissolve in all the mist,
Expose these things that don't exist,

Rise to darkness from the past,
To the light that did not last,

Brightly shone upon this earth,
To know the best to see the worst,

Tap, tap, tap, tap, tap, let me in,
I'm the secret from within,

Knock, knock, knock, knock, knock,
let me out,
I'm a secret to talk about,

I'm the truth from your youth,
Throughout your life I have no use,

Give me a moment of your time,
All my 'truths', you shall find,

Bring me to the surface floor,
Then your secrets will be no more,

Crystal clear as you shall see,
All the things revealed to me.

# It Might…

It might be deception,
They may make an exception,

They might change direction,
He may need protection,

They may feel rejection,
They may have connections,

There may be obligations,
They may have good relations,

There might be no communication,
It may be a dedication,

They might have an education,
Or perhaps a sensation,

They might've had a revelation,
To recognize the situation.

# **What it appears to be...**

Nothing's never what it appears to be,
Past experiences made a believer out of me,

I've experienced several types of illusions,
Which caused a circle of confusion,

I've spent priceless time trying to sort things out,
Never truly understanding what the situations were about,

I tried comprehending the things that I went through,
They were unimaginable as I'm describing them to you,

I was in predicaments that were scrutinized by others,
Yet, I defended its presence while rebelling against my
mother,

My perception of its reality led me to a block,
Scavenging through issues while I beg for them to stop,

I thought in my small concept it was pleasure,
Then my weakness evolved, into something unmeasurable,

My presence allows me to see things much clearer,
Once I walk-the-walk of deception, now I fear them,

# Dare to Change

You might process things differently after you've heard
from me,
It might change the course of your destiny,

Nothing is never what it appears to be,
Keep your 'mind' open, and you will be able to see.

# It is...

It is the heart to open for one to receive,
It is the mind to open for one to believe,

It is the 'will' to have for one to achieve,
It is the life to live for one to conceive,

It is the goal to reach for one to meet,
It is the dream to for fill for one to complete,

It is the work to be done for one to defeat,
It is the 'day' to be gone so bittersweet!

# What's Left...

Stability is what's left of unstable,

Security is what's left of insecurity,

Completion is what's left of defection,

Accomplish is what's left of incompetent,

Happiness is what's left from sadness,

Content is what's left from repent,

Deliverance is what's left from bondage,

Greatness is what's left from shortcomings,

Prosperity is what's left for misfortunes,

Wellness is what's left from sickness,

Companions is what's left from loneliness,

Friends is what's left from enemies,

# Dare to Change

Fulfillment is what's left from disappointment,

Acceptance is what's left from rejection,

Overflow is what's left from emptiness,

Blessings or what's left from depression,

Empathy is what's left from cruelty,

Belief is what's left from grief,

Success is what's left from failure,

Sanctification is what's left from
damnation,

Grace was given from God!
Mercy is what's left from Jesus!

# Black-Stripes…

All of your 'black stripes', against your 'white',
You'll have far to go to reach your light,

Stick out your chest hold up your head,
Your journey's long Lord Jesus said,

Swallow your pride let down your hair,
Your destiny is found everywhere,

All your 'black stripes', against your 'white',
Your faith will keep you strong during your fight,

Hold your tongue and keep your peace,
Jesus' love for you will never cease,

Go with God's love in your heart,
He'll give you the strength to do your part,

All your 'black stripes', against your white,
God sends His angels to protect your life,

Stand up to praise and kneel down to pray,
You'll receive God's blessings throughout your day,

# Dare to Change

48

Jesus died for our sins that's what I heard,
You'll find your comfort in God's word,

All your 'black stripes', against your white,
God will save your soul if you choose to live right.

# **Thanks for Giving...**

Thanks for giving,
Because you did more people are living,

The time and gifts that you share,
Let everyone know how much you care,

When you set aside your own personal needs,
To help others by doing good deeds,

Show the world your sensitive side,
By allowing your emotions to override,

Those that benefit is truly grateful,
This pleases God and for it I'm thankful,

It made the difference in so many lives,
It lightens their loads and help strengthen their fight,

You'll be truly blessed because you're given,
To help the unfortunate ones while you were living.

# **Comfort zone...**

I want to snatch you out of your comfort zone,
To let you know that you're not alone,

I'm going to bring to you some hardcore facts,
But, you must be willing to check yourself,

I want my message to gravitate,
Embrace my words don't hesitate,

Receive something that's heavenly meant,
Giving yourself the 'best', from it,

Now, hold on to that very thought,
Hear the truth come out my mouth,

Brace yourself and accept the fact,
Truth will always be the perfect match,

We all have flaws and baggage too,
Correct your own it's up to you,

You might have more, or you may have a few',
It all depends on what you do,

Step on out of your comfort zone,
To make it right, it won't be wrong.

## The Thrill of You …

Step into the thrill of you,
So you'll get to know you too,

Inside outside-outside in,
Come and get to know your best friend,

Help yourself to your own life,
Hold on tight it's your fight,

Riding through the atmosphere,
Check your ego don't you fear,

Embrace your qualities they are real,
They're here to bring you a whole new thrill,

Trust your instincts it's okay,
It's better to be yourself in every way,

Leave your doubts at the door,
There's no need to doubt any more,

Put yourself above all folks,
You're the one you need the most,

Dare to Change

52

Once trapped inside but now you're out,
Now show the world what you're about,

Now, you've gotten the thrill of you,
Now, you know just what to do.

# **Retrain Our Sons...**

Black men were born to be Kings, and breed to be
relentless,
Black men were strong warriors and also fearless,

They were born in a country with lots of wonders,
With mountains, jungles, and ferocious wild animals.

A large ship filled with "White men" came and stole them
from their ground,
They beat them mercilessly, and took their crowns,

The "White man", defiled them stripped them of their
heritage, and they were never the same,
They enslaved them and changed their names,

The mother's and wives watched their black men die before
their eyes,
When they refuse to conform, to the White men lies,

So, black mothers restrained their boys to be gentle and
sweet,
So, that the "masters", wouldn't kill off their entire sheep,

Did we make our black men lazy an inferior,
In order for the white man could feel superior,

# Dare to Change

We constantly showed them love, and gave them hugs,
We convinced them, their strength comes from above,

Now that we're no longer slaves,
We must retrain our sons, to be strong, and brave,

To come together as an invincible pack,
Stopping the racist "White men", in their tracks,

We build prisons of hell in our minds,
That's taking over our black men lives,

"The White Men" forced us to build prisons on the ground'
Then incarcerated our men and treated them remotely
profound,

Black mothers retrain your sons, so they don't end up in the
system,
Teach them the family values they're missing,

Teach them self-respect, and self-control,
So, when they reach adulthood they won't fold,

Set their standards for realistic goals,
Educate them to regain their self-control,

Mothers, and fathers, retain our black sons,
And, once again great leaders, they shall become.

# If I Could be…

If I could be a stepping stool for you to stand on my
shoulders, to the top of my head, in-order-to reach the
"Stars", then so be it,

But, when you have arrived, reach down, and pull me up to
allow me to see a star,

And I'll know, you've gone your distance,
Then my heart will be filled with content, and I've done
right by you.

# **Ruthless...**

Some people make crazy seem stupid,

Then afterwards they turn ruthless,

They think the world owes them something,
If they don't get paid, then they won't comprehend nothing,

They become rude and obnoxious,
Arrogant, disrespectful without, conscious,

They're always frustrated for no good reason,
There's no satisfying, or pleasing them,

They don't abide by any rules,
When you see them it's always bad news,

They always got something on their mind,
Trying to reason with them is a waste of time,

There is no need to make excuses,
Cause, these people will be forever 'ruthless'.

# On point…


Be on point with what you do,
Whatever you do will be appointed to you,

Give the best of what you have,
Then you'll always have the best to give,

Don't live your life through a dream,
But don't ever live your life without dreaming,

Search around to find a friend,
Make sure there's a friend to be found in you,

Sometimes you may not know where you want to go,
However, you'll know exactly where you need to be,

Never do too much to bring attention,
But always do enough to get attention,

Set your goals high in life,
You'll live up to your highest goals,

Keep things simple as can be,
Then things will be simply as they are,

Believe in something,
Then you'll have something to believe in,

# Dare to Change

Choose wisely,
Then you'll always make a wise choice,

Be responsible for your actions,
And be accountable for the things you're responsible for,

Have patience in life,
Wait on things in life patiently,

Do things purposely in life,
Then your life will always have
purpose,

Set goals in life,
As you reach them set more goals, to reach,

Be content with what you have,
What you have, will keep you content,

Grow higher in your achievements,
And you will achieve the highest,

Seek the truth in what you do,
And the truth will always come through you!

Notes with Purpose

## Notes with Purpose

Notes with Purpose

# Chapter 3

## *Gods Blessings*

# My 'Rock'...

Jesus, Jesus, Jesus, I need you,
In everything that I say, and everything I do,


The devil is trying to turn me against my children,
He wants my soul, and my life, to be ruined,


Help me Jesus, can't you see?
I'm praying for you, to set me free,


There's lots of things Lord, that I can't bare in my soul,
I'm asking You, to please take control,


My sense of direction can stop, on any day,
Lord please guide me, along the way,


From Genesis-2-Revelations,
Lead me to the 'rock', of my salvation,


You are my 'rock' that keeps me strong,
Never once have You left me on my own,


Thank You, Jesus, from being my 'rock',
I'll praise Your name-I will not stop.

# Overcome...

I can overcome all my obstacles,
Through Christ my Savior, anything's possible,

He gives me strength to carry on,
He died so I wouldn't be alone,

He carries my burdens when it's a heavy load,
He lifts my spirit and frees my soul,

He removed the shackles from my feet,
I share my story with the people I meet,

I give Him the glory throughout my day,
Because of it He blesses my praise,

In his word my faith is strong,
I open my heart as I sing my song,

He clears a path through my life,
He, tames my "enemy', in my fight,

He delivers me from all evil temptations,
He sends His 'blood', through each generation,

I can overcome the devil's 'wile',
Because, I know I am God's child.

## **Thank You Lord…**

Thank You, Lord thank You, Lord You've been my rock,
Please Lord don't You ever stop,

You've been so good Lord I thought they understood,
Thank You Lord, thank You Lord You've been so good,

You pick me up You turned me around,
You place my feet on solid ground,

Thank you, Lord, thank you Lord you've been my rock,
Please Lord don't you ever stop,

You kept me safe throughout my night,
You make sure, I wake to see your light,

Thank you, Lord, thank You Lord, You been so good to
me,
Thank You Lord, thank You Lord, You help me, so I can
see,

For all the blessings You've given me,
You been so good to me,

# Dare to Change

I just thank You Lord,
I thank You Lord, I thank You Lord.

You been my rock,
Please Lord don't you ever stop.

# God's Love...

I know how to be mad at someone,
But I don't know how to be mean to anyone,


Evil is mean and sometimes it's done for fun,

But love complies given by the 'Holy', one,

To bring us peace when He is done,


God will bring peace into your heart,
But you must believe in Him and do your part,


Trust in his 'word' from day to night,
He will bring deliverance, to your life,


God loves us so much, that he sent his only begotten son,
Because he did, our battles are already won,


God's gives us peace surpassing all of our understanding,
But he wants our free will-he won't demand it,

## Dare to Change


His love is mink, kindness and filled with blessings,
It comes through humility and sacrifices, during life
lessons,


God's love is honest, trustworthy, and won't fade away,
His love is dependable and reliable each and every day,


God's love is patience, and hardworking,
His love is determination with perseverance for certain,


God's love is courageous, stemmed with obstacles we've
endured,
God's love is today, tomorrow, and forever more!

# **Trick of the Devil...**


The devil is constantly trying to be slick,
By scheming and plotting with malicious tricks,


He's always trying to knock you off your square,
He vows to condemn you anywhere,


He sometimes comes with a friendly face,
Then your trust will be misplaced,


The devil will pretend to lend a helping hand,
To get you to drop your guards, it he can,


The devil comes in many disguises,
Some of which you're unable to recognize,


God will show you how to identify them,
If you keep your mind, stay on Him!


Stop allowing the devil to come into your mix,
Then you won't get caught up in his tricks.

# Not my fight...

I'm going to separate myself, from the equation,
And bring you something, that sure to amaze you,


All of the purities that God has sent,
A touch of 'heaven' when you repent,


God will forgive your 'sins', every time,
He'll renew your strength and victory you'll find,


He's a God of many chances,
You must choose to trust in Him-He won't demand it,


Leave all your burdens at the altar,
You'll be sure to find peace afterwards,


Some of your days may be challenging and even hard,
But, you must remember the battle's not yours, it's the
Lord's,

Through you may endure countless fights,

Each and every one of them will bring you closer to Jesus's
light,


So, if you're ever feeling lonely, or despair,
Just take a look around, your 'Savior's', everywhere.

# **Borrowed time...**

We're all on borrowed time,
If you could lend me a some of yours, I'll be fine,

We're only here for a little while,
Afterwards, we walk that 'mile',

We need to try and make the most of our entire lives,
By making good decisions and living wise,

Life's too short to be messing around,
After our parent's guidance then we're grown,

We need to make the best of our own situations,
By having a spiritual relation,

We must honor God and know that He's in control,
When we submit our lives to Him, He'll save our soul,

Try to live your life righteous and divine,
Because, we're all here on borrowed time.

# **Prayerful people…**

Prayerful people have more determination, with more
dedication,
They have less aggravation, with less frustration,

They're more likely to be at ease,
When they trust in God to satisfy their needs,

When their faith is strong,
They know that they're not alone,

They walk with Jesus during their days,
He strengthen them as they pray,

Their praises are for Our Father,
To call on His Holy Ghost Power,

When God fills their lives with His 'joy',
The world depressions they will avoid,

During their challenging times,
Jesus' peace they will find,

Dare to Change


74


If you're struggling during your day,
Talk to Jesus as you pray,


God will do the same for you,
As He's blessed the other believers too.

# Leave Your Burdens…

Leave your burdens at the cross,
Regardless of your worries God's the boss,

He sent His son to die and pay our cost,
He saved our souls, when His life was lost,

Challenges will come throughout our days,
But with our faith God won't allow them to stay,

Jesus was bruised for our iniquities,
In order gain our humility,

He was wounded for our transgressions,
To bring about Our Father's blessings,

Our chastisement of peace was amongst him,
To fill the world with Our Father's love,

Leave your burdens at the cross,
God will wash them clean just because.

# **Keep me Lord...**

Please Lord, take my hand when my time is near,
For I am Your loyal and faithful servant, and I shall not
fear,

Keep me strong in my final hour,
Linger near for it's You, I honor,

Keep my peace and allow the world to see,
So they will know I was humble as I could be,

Accept me Lord into Your gracious house,
I'll praise Your name when I open my mouth,

You are my 'King', at the time we shall meet,
I'll sing You Psalms and dance at Your feet,

Bless me Lord for I am Your child,
For I have suffered yet for a while,

When my time has come grant me relief,
For it is Your 'word', in my heart that brings me peace,

# Dare to Change

Keep me Lord in the comfort of your arms,
Where the world could no longer do me no harm,

Thank you, Lord, for all your grace,
While thy draw near as I see my 'Father's' face.

## **Sunshine…**

Sunshine in my life shining bright,
A reflection of God our 'Father', glorious light,

Brightening up my day and days to come,
Leaving me filled with Jesus' love,

Opening up doors for me to walk through,
Blessed to be with God's chosen few,

Empowered through Your beauty unlike no other,
Embracing my presence born through my mother,

Sunshine above all and one of a kind,
Brightly sparks in my life so wonderfully divine,

Sprinkling hope in my future with Your rays,
I thank God for Your presence with my praise,

Stay with my life throughout my time,
Flood my heart with Your 'sunshine'!

# A 'Reprobate' mind...

A 'reprobate' mind,
Rejected by God,

Beyond hope or salvation,
Without God's grace there is no consolation,

If you know what's right but it's not what you choose not to
do,
Then you'll be faced with God's wrath, set upon you,

If you are Christian then you know the right way,
Instead of doing what's right, you decide to stray,

God will forgive you over, and over again,
Except if you deny Him, and just continue to sin,

You'll be beaten with many stripes,
As you move further from God's light,

His salvation, you'll no longer find,
If He turns you over to a 'reprobate mind'.

# **Lord, you touched me…**

Lord, you touched me when no one else was there,
I was blessed by your presence because you care,

You gave me strength preceding everything,
You are my Savior, and also my King,

Lord, you blessed me, over and over again,
You are my deliver and also my friend,

Lord, you healed me on my sick bed,
You kept Your 'word', on every promise made,

Lord, You, gave me hope when all hope was lost,
When You sent Your only begotten son, to die upon the
cross,

Lord, You forgave me, for all of my sins,
After I repented, and allowed You, to come in,

Lord, You made a way for me when there wasn't a way,
Because of it I'm grateful each and every day,
Lord You opened doors for me to walk through,
Each step I made brought me closer to you.

# The Gift…

It's a woman going around,
Spreading poems throughout the town,

Exposing truth and stating facts,
Telling people about themselves,

God blessed her with insight,
To tell a story and tell it right,

She's bringing joy and a bit of cheer,
Though all the messages that you hear,

When you sit down to listen,
It makes you aware of what you're missing,

She has a special type of gift,
When you hear-your life will shift,

I don't believe it's actually planned,
Because she writes poems on demand,

She'll tell you if you mean or nice,
She'll write it once and read twice,

There's no need for attitude,
Her poems will surely change your mood,

# Dare to Change

She'll make you think and realize,
Respect the truth and not the lies,

The words are coming from her soul,
She's very wise but God's in control,

She's writes doing the day and during the night,
When she's done it's a big delight,

I'm very glad I heard her work,
When I started to laugh, it made her smirk,

If you haven't heard her yet,
You're in for a treat and that's a fact,

She has a lot of confident,
She'll make you cry she'll make you vent,

She's always willing to share her gift,
Making sure your mind doesn't drift,

She's has a lot of information,
To leave you with some inspiration,

So, come on over to listen-up,
The words she got will fill you up,

If I said it once I'll say it twice,
The poems she writes are very nice,

I never heard nothing so unique before,
It makes you want more, and more!

# **God's instructions…**

Sleep aid, muscle relaxers, and sleeping pills,
They're all just a man-made, cheap thrill,

Cause when God wants you woke, He'll wake you up,
There's nothing you can do so don't press your luck,

Give in to the 'spirit', when it comes your way,
Blessed will be your life with a brighter day,

God is trying-with love to get your attention,
Late in the midnight hour he wants you to listen,

He'll bring to you a very sacred message,
His words will be filled with your personal blessing,

Pay close attention to all of God's instructions,
He'll heal your body and relieve your suffering.

# **Your Own...**

God bless the child that has his own,
Your Grandma done told you,

Your Mama done show you,
When you get grown then you're on your own,

You must pay your bills in your home,
Or, you won't have one for very long,

You'll be left on the streets to roam,
Left without a place to call your own,

To keep the things which you belong,
Down you're feeling sad, and all alone,

So, you called a friend on the phone,
But, there weren't any left, they were all gone.
Safe and warm in their homes,

However, whenever you call on God you're never alone,
He will always protect you and keep you strong.

# Stand on Your Own…

May God forgive me if I'm wrong,
I just yell at you to keep you strong,

Because one day I'll be gone,
Then you'll be left to stand on your own,

Hear my voice while I'm gone,
It will keep you safe and it'll keep you strong,

When you're in doubt of what to do,
Find the courage to own your truths,

Know my love was meant for you,
May God be with you to see it through!

## Notes with Directions

## Notes with Directions

Notes with Directions

88

9 781954 308503